It Was A
Short Summer,
Charlie Brown

It Was A Short Summer,

Charlie Brown

Charles M. Schulz

SCHOLASTIC BOOK SERVICES

New York Toronto London Auckland Sydney Tokyo

ISBN 0-590-30059-8

21 20 19 18 17 16 15   2 3 4/8

On the first day of school, the assignment given to the class was to write a five-hundred-word theme on what they did during the past summer. Linus raised his hand and asked, "How do you teachers keep coming up with these great new ideas?"

That evening, Charlie Brown tried to work on his theme and soon found it to be harder than he had thought. "1-2-3-4-5-6-7-8 — 492 words to go.

"Sigh."

English theme... TITLE...
"What I did This Summer"
This summer I went
to camp.

Linus wasn't doing too much bet-
ter, but he remembered how the summer began.

"Hey! Great news! Guess what!! I've just signed everyone up for summer camp."

"Camp? Everyone?"

"Absolutely," declared Lucy. "There's to be no discussion and you needn't feel it necessary to thank me."

"Camp?!" shrieked Linus. "You won't catch me going to any summer camp. They always have those camps out in the woods

some place and those woods are full of queen snakes. Have you ever been chomped by a queen snake, Charlie Brown? Boy, you get chomped by a queen snake and you've had it. You won't get me near any woods full of queen snakes. No sir, not me!"

Lucy said, "I'll tell all the parents that each one of you is happy to go."

"AAUGH!!"

In spite of the complaints, all of the kids showed up at the bus depot the next day . . .

and Snoopy included himself in the
invitation. He seemed to have more
baggage than everyone else.

He was very enthusiastic about the trip and even tried out the bus driver's seat just to see what it would be like to drive such a huge vehicle.

The boys had a terrible time getting into the bus, but the girls, under the direction of Peppermint Patty, formed a line and marched very smartly up the steps. Lucy, being sort of in charge of everything, had made Peppermint Patty her No. 1 assistant.

The camp turned out to be a very nice place with wooden-framed tents on each side of a small lake. The boys settled down in one set of tents and the girls in the other.

Charlie Brown tried to give a dem-
onstration on bed-making, but it
wasn't very good. Snoopy, however,
showed them how to make a bed so
tight that you could bounce a quarter
on it.

The first camp activity was a swimming challenge which pitted the boys against the girls.

The boys swam like they were still climbing into the bus, and the girls had no difficulty at all beating them out to the raft and back. It was a crushing defeat for the overconfident boys, but Charlie Brown tried to cheer them up by saying, "Don't be discouraged, it isn't like we lost a ball game or something really important.

In fact," he continued, "that gives me an idea. Why don't we challenge the girls to a softball game? We know we could beat them playing ball." This didn't turn out to be true, however, for the girls, led by Peppermint Patty's great hitting, easily defeated the boys, which made them more discouraged than ever.

That night they sat around the campfire, toasting marshmallows and feeling sorry for themselves.

Snoopy had his own special method.

In fact, Snoopy sort of led a life of his own, making his own meals and sleeping in a little tent by himself.

The competition continued the next day when Roy came running up to Charlie Brown and said, "Hurry, Charlie Brown, they're having a canoe race."

"We'll show them, Snoopy," said Charlie Brown. We'll get in this canoe and we'll win this race and we'll be heroes."

Paddling furiously, he said,

"We're going to win this canoe race, Snoopy, or die trying."

"I'm going to paddle, and paddle and paddle."

About five minutes later, however, he collapsed from exhaustion, but then suddenly sat up and said, "I wonder if we won."

"No," declared Roy, "but you got four feet from the dock." Now Charlie Brown himself was dejected.

"If there was only some way we could beat the girls at something." And then he noticed Snoopy and Linus doing a little arm wrestling and it suddenly came to him that this might be the answer. "Boy! Why didn't I think of this before?"

He gathered all the boys around a table and said, "I propose that we issue a challenge to those girls across the lake to have a wrist-wrestling contest. The masked marvel here will be our champion."

Snoopy immediately began doing exercises to prepare himself for the <u>big</u> event.

The girls, of course, readily accepted the challenge and put forth Lucy as their champion. It looked like it was going to be a great match.

The two contestants faced each other at the corner of a table and locked hand and paw.

They strained with all their might and glowered fiercely at each other, but neither could seem to put the other's arm down.

Suddenly, Snoopy leaned across the table and kissed Lucy on the nose.

"FOUL!! FOUL!!" she cried. "This stupid masked marvel fouled.

"I'm the winner.

"I won."

"So in conclusion," Linus wrote in his theme, "I must say that it was a difficult summer."

"I got an A on my vacation paper, Charlie Brown," said Linus. "What did you get?"

"I got a C—."

"It was kind of a short summer, wasn't it, Charlie Brown?"

"Yes," said Charlie Brown, "and it looks like it is going to be a long winter."